THE
SWARM

THE SWARM

Dalia Neis

THE ELEPHANTS

Published 2022 by The Elephants
Book design by Aimee C. Harrison
Author photo by Dalia Neis
The text of this book is set in Plantin MT Pro
22 23 24 25 26 5 4 3 2 1
First Edition

ISBN 978-1-63955-104-0 (print) and
978-1-63955-105-7 (ebook)

Library of Congress Control Number 2022944340

for Friedush Bulzan

Contents

Part Two.   The Owl & the Gazelle

Part Three.   Into the Carpathians

They gathered on the great Path as one
voice, comrades in longing, and said:
Hoopoe, bird of experience, how are we
to manage this flight?
—*Farid ud-Din Attar*

▽ ▽ ▽   This film was intended to be screened in Technicolor on the autumnal equinox at an outdoor auditorium at Kryvorivnya, the Carpathian village where Sergei Parajanov filmed *Shadows of Forgotten Ancestors.*

▽ ▽ ▽   I was instructed to make this film by a secret anarcho-revolutionary order inspired by the *Chernoe Znamia* revolts in Białystok where the members gathered by the bartak trees in the forest of Bacieczkowski, screaming like jackals at night, terrifying tyrants and landowners.

▽ ▽ ▽   There are no main protagonists in this film, quite simply because my memory is incapable of chronicling the multitude.

▽ ▽ ▽   There is an ever-growing cast of actors.

▽ ▽ ▽   We began as an intimate gathering of friends and lovers in the thermal baths of Budapest.

▽ ▽ ▽   With the four winds on our back, we operated from our head-quarters, which included the Bambi Ezpresso Bar in Buda, the sprawling landscape of the streets of Budapest, the Ottoman thermal baths, and the sewage system of Pest. From thereon we departed the depths of the Danubian basin for the western Carpathian peaks.

▽ ▽ ▽   With the aid of the flock of birds who joined our great army, we became a thin layer of crust that molted on the soft grounds of Budapest.

▽ ▽ ▽   This is a vampire tale. We are vampires in the making: not the kind that digs into flesh but the ones who swoop into the dimensions of vamplore which pre-empt the origins of family and the confines of conjugality. When the regime tries to smell us, we give off another scent. To the advanced human we bestow a scent of cum, and to the imbeciles, rotten flesh.

▽ ▽ ▽   We are the geological membranes that have lined the depths of the city's springs.

▽ ▽ ▽   We obeyed the instructions of the Dacian queen, the fleeting glamour of the Habsburg, and the specters of Bektashi Sufism that slipped through the cracks of the Ottoman years. We learned the arts of medicinal protection by the summoning of thermal water spirits, and by the homoerotic act of bathing in darkened chambers steamed with rose water.

▽ ▽ ▽   We botched a robbery at the National Bank of Hungarian Trade. They sent police with machine guns, we dodged the bullets, and sailed into the Danube before flying through a gap in the Carpathian gates.

Part One   The Danube Dwellers

If not now, when?
—*The Király Baths*

This is the eye of Budapest. Bathing in this medieval Ottoman Bath. Strange city with shadows of fascism old and new, hot springs with volcanic charge. The thermal springs belong to the earth's core, not to the state. Fascism seems to dissipate here. Hard not to feel softened by the filtered lights, refracted from the pin-pricked, domed roof, the lucid glow in the bathers. Perhaps the same lucidity that infiltrated the octagonal, quiet, sensual chamber built by Ottomans who smuggled the eroticism of geometric knowledge, which swept thru the sites of optical pioneers in medieval al-Andalus, or the circular beauty of the Bektashi dervishes drowning in the beloved's path.

This is the eye of Budapest. All knowledge can be found here. There are hot springs of sulphate and sodium; a steamed room of rose oil ... I feel them looking at me ... it feels good. This is my synagogue, my mosque. I read *The Conference of the Birds*. I'm contemplating flight. What flight means here and what it means to flee. Hungary is taking a delirious turn to the right. I am in this odd bubble at the CEU, an artist in residence, a more glamourous name for temporary adjunct faculty. They let me be a filmmaker as long as I teach, but the CEU has been dismantled by the government in their George Soros witch hunt.

There is a magical ley line stretching from my 1950's guesthouse, in the hills of Buda, up to the tomb of Gül-Baba, the Bektashi dervish, on Rózsadomb, and winding down past the cinema at the crossroads of the Danube and the Király Bathhouse on Fő utca to the Soviet Espresso Bar, Bambi, where I spend my time reading while old men play draughts. I caught one of them glaring at me. Maybe it was because I was reading *Our Death* by Sean Bonney? As an Ashkenazi whose ancestors come from these parts, I pass. But they may have guessed that I am not one of them. They may have seen one of my horns. Perhaps Bonney's book sent them talismanic curses.

The hum grows, at first imperceptibly among the bathers' babble, and then more distinctly, in polyphonic splendor as my body lies cradled under the shooting fountain of spring water. I will continue reading *The Conference of the Birds* and plot an inverted uprising in this cruising den of mist and steam amid the backdrop of the holy hum. Then I need to meet the Danube Dwellers. Then I will figure out why I must denounce my origins.

"Did you hear?"

"They escaped across the burial mound."

"The forbidden zone."

"Climbed over the fence at night & broke into the crypt."

"Five women with five vaginas."

"They are not women & never have been."

"They are no longer human."

☙·❀·❧

Oh you foolish little Zionists
With your utopian mentality
You'd better go down to the factory
And learn the worker's reality
You want to take us to Jerusalem
So we can die as a nation
We'd rather stay in the Diaspora
And fight for our liberation
—Anonymous Yiddish ditty (1931)

I was falling asleep to a lecture on the Holocaust. Yeah, I know
it's heretical, but holocaust humor goes back to my childhood
and a habitual fatigue at the H word was quite common in my
parts. Holocaust humour opens wallowing self-pity into trans-
formative potential, with seeds of revolutionary empathy for
all underdogs across space and time. My father and his family
are Transylvanian Jews. Aside from my grandparents, the only
relative to survive was my aunt Friedush, who died recently in
Oradea at the age of 103. She miraculously survived the war by
marrying a militant communist. I grew up with stories of ances-
try, superstition, belief, and war.

Before I lost my courage and became a tedious TV documen-
tary filmmaker, I made experimental films about these stories.
Filmed in the Czech Republic, my super-8 film *Bike Ride* was
about a girl's first bike ride to Theresienstadt: she cycles in a

trance state from a tunnel in Prague into sand dunes, across an abandoned motorway, and straight into the gates of "Arbeit Macht Frei." I smashed on the soundtrack, a detuned, slowed-down rendition of Debussy by the Japanese composer Isao Tomita. Shot on just one and half roles of super-8 film, the film had a road movie quality, almost epic.

My later short film, "Goray 1648", was about the seventeenth century false messiah, the Sabbatai Zevi, who sent his messenger, Nathan of Gaza, to the impoverished village of Goray—the village of my maternal ancestors. Nathan seduced the community into an ecstatic frenzy. Ablutions and secret sexual acts were performed and intoxicating nights of dancing and singing ensued. He convinced the community to take flight to the promised land where they would find riches awaiting them. As they were about to board their boats, news swept through the village that he had been sent on behalf of a false messiah, the Sabbatai Zevi, who had converted to Islam. *Goray 1648* drew on this story and mashed up scenes from Yiddish cinema, nineteenth century painted postcards of Palestine, and animations of talismanic spells. An apocalyptic horror film, it charted a community's ecstatic dreams and delirious hope for a promised land, from messianic doom to settler colonialism: an attempt to rethink Walter Benjamin's angel of history through the archives, in the form of a crazed, looping folktale.

"Yad Vashem"—the speaker's voice suddenly rose to an impassioned pitch—"the memory of the holocaust, a museum built on the earth of the promised land." But whose promise and to whom?

"The museum's architecture," the speaker continued, pointing to grey squares on a corporate screen "is split between the museum entrance, chronicling the Jewish genocide to the grand liberation finale, corresponding to the exit at the botanical gardens, a symbol of a nation's salvation and return to the homeland."

Here I was, supposedly surrounded by comrades. But what were we united against?

In Białystok, 1905, the Chernoe Znamia, an anarcho-communist brigade, conducted secret meetings in a forest on the outskirts of town. Their idea was to resist the pogroms and the nationalist uprisings, and continue to live as a radical free people, uprooted and nomadic. What hailed the jackal cries that brought down the tyrants of 1905?

Napszállta: The Veli Bej Baths (Women's Night)

On a Friday evening in 1913, sparrows circled the Veli Bej baths twenty-seven times. In 2019, László Nemes filmed *Napszállta*, where it's 1913: the hat factory, the riot, the ensuing collapse of the Austro-Hungarian empire. The Jewess wanders in and out of the frame. Budapest is bathed in a golden luminous light. The field of vision is tightened, only the Jewess in frame leads us through the city's labyrinths, to the resistance fighters, to her persecutors. The light spills in, the city around her is out of focus. We make abstract shapes from the forms of the city. The Hapsburg empire is about to burst. Here, emerging from this pool of light, the Danube Dwellers arrive. We can hear the faint hum fade in. Its sound enters our field of vision as moving shards of golden light.

On that Friday evening eighty-five years later, the sparrows circled around the Veli Bej baths twenty-seven times. The Jewess has disappeared, and the Hapsburg empire vanished in the shadow of the Ottoman years. There are sparrows and owls, pigeons and crows. I saw them fly up in the sky as they swooped above the bath, swirling and cackling. They flew in a sharp line southward.

"Do you love me?"

                                                         "Yes."

"Then avoid the shrunken reporter at all costs.
He may seem like a comrade, but he is not.
His heart is hardened and made of lead."

          "Send him down the wrong alley. There are simulated
alleys, alleys within alleys. Go to the Rudas baths on
women's night. You will enter the Finnish sauna and
there you will find the mute Shoshoah. Don't get a
hard on. Just sit calmly beside her and ask for her name.
After she signs her name, you must gaze at her until
you lose yourself and disappear into the cracks of the
sauna's drain pipes. From there, you will need to swim
for a while; don't be put off by the stench of the sew-
age nor the glare of the Dwellers Dwellers, but keep on
until you are thrust from the hot springs into the river."

"Once the great forces spit you out of the Danube,
 go immediately to the Bambi Ezpresso Bar in Buda,
 our headquarters."

> "You'll find Rekas and Ilona sitting on the red
> faux leather sofa facing east. They will be reading
> a book of verse by the Hungarian factory
> worker and dissident, József Atilla."

"When they mouth the word *MINDEN*
 ("EVERYTHING"), buy them three plum Palinkas."

> "Wait for them to get drunk, agree to walk them home."

"Don't get a hard on, and don't ask them
 to make love, not yet."

ŏ·ℚ·ŏ

"This is all bigger than you," mimed the mute Shoshoah,
"bigger than your sex drive and bigger than desire
itself. The Danube Dwellers are just molecules, phan-
toms, and alien stars that evaporate in your organs the
moment you stretch your hands out to receive the change
for your *Amerikai Hosszú Kávé*. You can acknowledge
the Danube Dwellers or ignore them, but you must feel
them first. They are forces helping you to escape."

"At midnight we will all meet by the tomb of Gül Baba on Rose Hill. Banshee has a key to the crypt."

Barzakh: The Intermedial Dimension

It was soft, like the entrails of a peacock, or softer still, velvet to the touch. I felt it in my hands, caressed and kissed its ears. They told me to leave it be, that I must move in the direction of sobriety. And I am sober, for I don't drink, but I heard the voices of the dead speak in my mouth. In my voice they told me the secret of the birds' flight and encouraged me to leap from staircases in shopping malls and from elevator stands. As a child, doctors prescribed Guanfacine to calm my mind. Nevertheless my imagination roamed thousands of miles, and centuries back and forth. They sedated me with Guanfacine, but I was too restless to be tied with a straitjacket of the mind. I lived in the far-future, and embodied a past more remote than my great-great-grandmother. I saw her forlorn beneath a thunderstorm, unaware that she would die under the fallen branch of an oak tree. I heaved myself up the branches and clasped the owl in my hand. It was an eagle owl, almost as tall as my waist. Its eyes were brighter than the whites of my own eyes, and yellow, and neon, bigger than my growing skull. I kissed its beak and softly asked for consultation.

In the libraries of the city, I delved into their manuscripts, books that, where it was perceived as a blessing of the saint rather than a curse of a demon, revealed how I might hear the voices. For whether I were instructed by a demon or benign spirit, I knew life was elevated when the imagination was set free. The flight of the imagination was all that mattered to me, and it wasn't a mere aesthetic problem or a question of formalism. It was about slipping into the intermedial dimension, where dreams are given the respect that they deserve as compass points of the heart. And I was born with a broken heart, a tormented familial tree. They told me to place objects on the altar. The altar was to become an anti-tree, where a bark and a stone and a feather would melt the roots within me.

Later, after the pleading voices of my formative years quieted, I became a filmmaker who made linear documentaries. They were as dull as any other television investigation, perhaps even duller than those. I tackled all sorts of "subjects" on "controversial topics" and "taboos." But nothing is taboo if you use a language that cannot speak for you. I was into Andrey Tarkovsky, yes, and even Maya Deren, sure, but that didn't help. Neither did the privilege of film school or the cinephilic ardor of my youth. I, Dali Muru, was once a respected filmmaker who made boring documentaries, and I was often called upon to present myself at these primarily white, cis-male, European documentary panels. I was a mentor for other filmmakers who were more inspired than I was, for I was jaded. But now I'm making sense, because life then made so much sense, so much sense that it drove me mad. The baths, and the Carpathians, saved my life.

"Are you a Judeo-Islamic water cult?"

"This is sorcery. We take all the resources on offer to us. Bektashism is one of them; the baths another."

"For what purpose?"

"It's a homeopathic necessity. It's the fucking Middle Ages here. We are even prepared to whistle the secret code of the Silbo Gomero to slip through the cracks."

The Jinn of Genealogies

Sorcerers always count events in sets of threes. But first I must paint the scenes leading to the Bektashi bath apparition: nothing extraordinary at first, the bathers' faces were blurred and foggy, and there was the soothing murmur and babble of flowing spring water.

Before arriving, I was in Satu Mare, on my way to Budapest after a trip into the Carpathians. We were making a film about my ancestral roots for Czech TV, but our cameras were stolen and we were, in any case, too absorbed by the journey itself to continue making the film. My desire for her felt like a great bulb from one of those baboon plants that leap suite to spa to hornbeam along the horizontal expanse on the Transylvanian plateau. We were in the Hattyu Street cemetery in Oradea, lost and eaten by large mosquitos. We were searching for my aunt's tombstone.

The tombstones were beaten to dust by the fascists and worn out by centuries of neglect. The caretaker brought out the manuscript of the dead and laid it on the wooden table in front of his disheveled shack, the weeds growing sideways as stray dogs barked in the twilight air. The pages twitched and turned in the wind while the caretaker began to recite the names of the dead. From each corner of the burial site, dogs barked before stealthily venturing to the cemetery's center, where they sat atop broken stones and chewed on discarded bones.

She filmed the pages blowing in all directions, and I thought how this would make a strikingly gothic cinematic scene (or, at least a highly effective incantation film). But very quickly we were gone, never to return. We jumped on the next bus to Maramures, elated and restless from our love-filled, turbulent night on the threshold of Lion's Gate. After the first night in the presidential suite, because I insisted on nothing less than royal treatment after the way my family were treated by the SS, we awoke to beetles and bugs flying over our silk covers, crawling on the walls and lampshades, dead on our pillowcases. This is what the nouveau riche, what aristo-dreams are made of: when you want royalty you get the insects. If that's good in general, not so tonight, no, not for a night of love in the post-SS, post-Soviet world of Oradea. I wanted royalty, and demanded it on the cheap! 20 *leus* and two arguments with the receptionist later, we won the actual bona fide presidential suite, bug free, and with a balcony that out-stretched onto the grand square below.

The next day after one too many goulash soups, and smoked duck and cheap egg salad with lemon toast that glistened in a crystal glass with silver teaspoons studded with faux diamonds, my love for her spilled, and expanded, racing beyond any inverted desire for reconnecting with the broken roots of my family tree. I was meant to visit my uncle Kiki, the son of my great-aunt Friedush. I loved Friedush, and though I had great admiration for her stoicism and incredible nose for survival, it was a relief to leave my roots behind and move laterally, into the space of the Carpathians. It was as though what was needed was merely a brief backward glance in order to face the other direction, the panoramic, and move forward until origins disappear.

I read these thoughts in an eighteenth century Bretonian sorcery manual: that the dissolution of personal identity and familial trees was a prerequisite for abstract flight. This seemed to echo the words of Shoshoah, Banshee, Ilona, and Rekas, in their instructions for me to perform these anti-origin rituals.

Shadows of Forgotten Ancestors

In my head, I could hear the Sergei Parajanov drymba soundtrack of *Shadows of Forgotten Ancestors* as we travelled higher into the Carpathians. Parajanov kept moving. That was his trick. He was a troubadour who circumvented cultural baggage. No one could claim him. In Armenia, he was a national idol. In Georgia, too. In Kryvorivnya, the Hutsul village where we were headed to, he was key cinematic witness to a vanishing world expunged by Stalin. He dipped in and out of the Caucuses like a travelling salesman, smuggling film reels in his suitcase and excavating minor languages across the Carpathians. In the bus, eurotrash on the radio gave way to a freewheeling mixtape in my head. We drove past local tourist resorts and faded Soviet hotels, now empty and forlorn where families once came in droves. Inflation meant the *hryvnia* currency bestowed us a privilege I couldn't fathom. It was affordable to eat three bowls of borscht, slow cooked by a *bouba* in the kitchen, full of slow-cooked nutrition we needed badly. The Carpathians rose and heaved between valleys. They were there, in the background, when we crossed the Tysa into Transcarpathia, and now they enveloped us. We circled up into the first mountain range and my head felt lighter. I caught yellow mountain flowers tremoring from the corner of my eye. The Carpathians came from the future. They amplified a shepherd's tone, the circular overtones of the *drymba* sending waves of cattle through the valleys, an almost secret gateway to the sky, to a mode of lightness, and to relief from the baggage of history.

Parajanov opened a line of flight in *Shadows of Forgotten Ancestors,* with its tragi-ecstatic evocation of a transpersonal, elemental time. It was supposed to be a Hutsul adaptation of *Romeo and Juliet.* Romantic. Yet it opened a crack into the future; the Carpathian space was so charged that it transformed domestic tragedy into impersonal romance . One place turned into another. A human became an animal. The wedding scene mutated into an eerie dance of beasts.

What would a polymorphic, vampiric, Transcarpathian remake of *Shadows of Forgotten Ancestors* look like, sound like? We moved through gothic, Dracula territory to reach the transcendental outside. Inter-special sexual liaisons were very common here. One could see it in the trees, and in the smell of the wild flowers on the mountain peaks. The wolves sounded different. We all know that we are here for a reason. I began to visualize, in abstract, animated forms, the nomadism of a people, the development of new lines of trans-migrational species crossing river paths and streams, into the plains and valleys and gushing down peninsulas to the water. I am not a nature freak and this is no messianic dirge. This is not travel writing. *She saw the structure and patterns of movement,* said a voice from nowhere.

The Filmmaker's Fall to Grace

It's a cinephile's wet dream to sail the Danube, reach the peak of the Carpathians, and enter the Hutsul village where Parajanov filmed *Shadows of Forgotten Ancestors*. The fact that we never arrived there stripped it down to a merely tantric gesture. Vorokhta. One village away from Kryvorivnya. A mere twenty minutes' drive up the Makivka mountains. But we arrived a fraction of a moment too late; the shamanic ski trainer was already asleep, for he had risen at the crack of dawn to pick herbs in the upper valley. I succumbed to this detour. The unfilmable ran through our lives with a vivid tenacity. This was no ordinary pilgrimage; my libido softened. There was a lightness in my sexual tract. My blue-flamed desire was captured by mountain awe, only to be cooled down by mugwort leaves.

Shoshoah was elated by this report. It felt sacred to be here, on this plateau, with these people. We stayed overnight at a *dacha* dorm beside a medieval wooden chapel. Everything smelled slightly metallic, as though Chernobyl fumes still lingered in the drain pipes. The mountains in the windows glanced back at us indifferently, and we could hear wolves close by. I held her closely. It wasn't meant as an invitation to sex. I was overcome with love for this place, for her, and for the others. We fell asleep amid a curious collective bodily intertwinement, moving toward each other in a state of diffused joy. Again, I dreamed of ancestors. They came from a rare squirrel family who were pushed by giant hyenas to the edge of a precipice, where they survived two ice ages by wedding rocks to trees.

I was drawn to her in the way that a soul desires to take flight in another person's body, or when you feel your love impersonally reverberate in the landscape. She went back to Budapest from Sighetu to meet her boyfriend. This would be our last moment of sweetness before an unspeakable rupture and terrifying reversal. No amphetamines, no therapy, just Golden Teachers for me, and micro-doses every other day. But the floodgates opened and it became too much. In the afterglow of our final embrace, in that hotel room in Sighetu, I experienced a joy so vast that I managed to sit through a five-hour bus ride back to Budapest despite a spurt of food poisoning from a former Soviet cantine in Satu Mare.

Weakened, with an empty stomach, I went straight to the baths. I went to the Király Fürdő, the oldest bath and the least frequented by tourists. I could hear the hum faintly at first and then, by my third day in the baths, more distinctly. It had rich vocal overtones, like transmission recorded at slow speeds, as if the static of the voices were serrated by some kind of technological glitch. The humming seemed to originate in the cracks of the stone-walled chamber, from the eroding medieval drainpipes that came up from the hot spring core, through Triassic carbonate rock. We'd follow the hum's source from the Transcarpathian basin up to the Carpathian plateau. Bom Bom Bow!

"They love to dwell in dampness."

"Do they cause harm?"

"They are neither good nor bad."

"You dragged your depleted body and spirit to the baths. Your channels were wide open for them to enter into you."

"How do you maintain your heart in the face of adversity?"

"Grief, anger and pity tie knots in the soul. If you stay soft, they will heal, the bats will heal, the baths will heal you."

I dived down to the bottom of the bath and saw that Ilona, Shoshoah and Rekas had hooves for feet. The better-than-us creatures were upon us.

Was It the Babble of the Bathers
or the Murmur of the Bath Spirits?

The doctors said I experienced an audio hallucination, due to the hexagonal-domed architecture of the bathhouse and its languid, disorientating space. The walls were thinned by erosion and I grew delirious when I heard a hum that morphed into insatiable vast voices, transformed into owls and a ghazellian form of antiquity. Was it the babble of the bathers or the murmur of the bath spirits? For voices have been heard in these parts—yeah, Orbán—and all voices are adrift in the state of disharmony. My Bektashi bath syndrome was in fact the awareness of a sonic presence, acousmatic voices, speaking from the depths of the Danube across time and space.

Three moons away from Lockdown, at the Pushkin Cinema, I watched *Fehérlófia*, a 1981 Hungarian animation in Technicolor about a horse goddess who gives birth to a humanoid named Treeshaker who is sent to the underworld to slay dragons, and where he encounters a gnome in seven colors with a beard as long as a hoe. Treeshaker can't shake off his gravity and tried to slay the barks of the tree that kept him from moving freely. The image of the horse goddess travelling in the forests of antiquity, pre-nation state Hungary, when the Danube met the Carpathians without interruption, a cathartic expression of the great conjunction of Jupiter and Saturn.

The sound of prehistoric synth lines and jew harps morphed into amplified galloping hooves. This is all I could do to make the movie about the *al-gayb*, the unseen, about the hum—it's a road movie at best and a tepid horror at worst (if you define the horror genre by twists and turns, that is). The nuts and bolts of the motor that push the narrative forward, as if ejaculating the protagonist into the unknown, screeching toward some kind of break in the action, some solace under the dappled leaves of an eucalyptus tree. It's worse than the fragments of a Daphne de Maurier screenplay, for even within these fragments, you can find clues, preludes to the mystery solved, sung in chords of fuzzy synth lines.

The fuzzy synth line said that Gül Baba was trying to heal me. The *qirya* summoned the jinn and jinnea in an effort to circumvent my origins. Then the *whaa wa* of a guitar, with some reverb effect pedals picked up from the secondhand shop in Rákóczi útca, clashed with syncopated dissident dervishes twisting down the bath hall, and the film ended disappointingly with a smattering of bird sounds as an effect of ambient authenticity. Yet the hum remained, pitched down to a polyphonic drone, before splintering out into the streets of Buda: Bom Bom Bow!

"The cleaner is called Eszter.
 She holds the keys to all the baths."

        "She also holds a spare key to Gül Baba's crypt."

"How do I approach her?"

        "Leave offerings of *keke* and oranges at the tomb."

"Complement her hairdo."

        "Tip her generously after bathing."

Oy Vey iz Mir!: The Rudas Baths (Women's Night)

Tremors come from underground. You can feel it walking the streets of Buda, particularly near the crossroads which stretch toward Margaret Bridge to the east and Rose Hill to the south, where thermal waters foam up from the Boltív spring at the foot of the Rózadomb. The path from Bambi to Gül Baba makes me giddy. Spring water circulates from the Transdanubian basin into the carbonate Triassic rock, and its discharge sends nearly imperceptible shivers up to the surface.

Even Pest has the tremors. The tomb of Gül Baba is illuminated, and one can see the crescent moon shining on the hill. Dormant and gushing thermals, pent up and stirring. I'm fed up with the fascist turn, and the impending threat of familial conjugality. Why did they think that I was married to this philosophy fellow just because I was standing next to him at the board meeting? FFS. I am in love with Rekas, Banshee, Shoshoa, Ilona Elek, and the wives of the fellows. Some aren't human, and some are liminal beings that follow the flight of sparrows. I would rather shack up with them. There are a thousand imperceptible earthquakes erupting in this city every millisecond.

My stomach is bloated after eating too much *káposztás tészta*, a brutal peasant dish of green cabbage and a squared pasta fried in butter and honey and garnished with coarse black pepper. My grandparents used to prepare it for me as a child. I ate it when I visited Aunt Friedush in Transylvania.

Professor X, a communist comrade from the CEU, promised to cook it for me. It tasted slightly different, a bit heavier and a bit sweeter. Perhaps the honey and the type of cabbage made a difference. Everything tastes richer here. Perhaps my taste buds have expanded. The aftertaste of paprika. The acidic warmth of plumed *palinka*. The explosive fire at the back of my throat. I worry I will put off the bathers, especially Rekas, Shoshoah and Ilona, who are bathing tranquilly beside me. But for whatever reason they appear more enamored with me than ever, brushing up close to me, flicking my earlobes, and stroking my scalp.

The Strange Swordplay of Ilona Elek

As taught by the two-sticked acrobat, Tysza Ramkuna

I promised Banshee that I'd visit the tomb of the interwar fencing champion, Ilona Elek, which lies on the hills of Buda in the Farkasréti Cemetery. I knew that by when she asked me to *visit*, Banshee really asked me to *summon*. I was to summon Ilona Elek.

Ilona Elek knew the art of martial navigation via the sword and, the decade when the Nazis banned her from competition notwithstanding, she won three Olympic gold medals.

Ilona Elek had learned the art of swordplay from an elderly woman named Tysza Ramkuna, whom she met on Sas-hegyi Látogatóközpont (Eagle Hill) in 1924. The hill's vast precipice was known for inhabiting a kingdom of rare Pannonian lizard: a sprawling green rocky crevice with granite caves, towering over a bourgeois neighbourhood of marble mansions and gaudy embassies. Up on the peak, one could see a panorama of Budapest—Pest sprawled out into the abyss, the Danube a snake-shifting form, widening, and thinning across the crest of the city, and Buda—with its multiple hills, the Gellért, Jánoshegy, Széchenyi-hegy, and farther north, on a clear day, all the way out to Tranyslvania and the steaming Carpathian peaks.

One early spring morning, Ilona Elek, then a wild teen with an excessive abundance of restless energy, climbed to the top of the hill and observed an elderly woman making curious movements with a pair of wooden sticks; she'd paint the sky with her hands, tracing the flight of birds, then point to the ground below her feet, as if tracing the microscopic movements of ants. The sticks seemed endowed with a life force of their own.

Tysza Ramkuna pierced the clouds and brought the rain. Sometimes she'd arch her stick to the sun and bring forth the fiery energy of summer. If she wanted snow, she'd swivel her hips north to Transylvania and summon the last traces of winter. The most joyful moment to behold was to see Tysza Ramkuna trace the migration of birds towards the Carpathians. The birds themselves would sweep, circularly, in time with the movements of the woman's sticks, chiming with the patterns of her spiraling gestures through their song.

One morning, Ilona Elek saw Tysza Ramkuna hanging upside down from a peach tree on a lower slope down the hill. Holding her two sticks beneath her, she looked like a bat. Her white hair streamed down like a witch's broomstick. 'So that is an *acrobat*,' thought Ilona Elek.

The old woman let out a yelp and, as she hung upside down from the branch, a trail of iridescent butterflies flew out of her mouth, hovering to and fro.

Tysza Ramkuna must have been very old. Her face was deeply wrinkled. She would later reveal to Ilona Elek that she was one hundred and two, and that she used to first be a tightrope walker, then a sword swallower, and that her travelling acrobat troop was one of the oldest in Hungary, dating back to the Hapsburg empire, run by a Bektashi magician who entertained King Suleiman the Great.

Tysza Ramkuna taught Ilona Elek to draw on the sky with the sticks—tracing the flight of birds and the constellation of the stars.

In the morning, they drew the migration of birds to Transylvania.

At noon sun, they would draw the movement of Pannonian lizards.

At dusk, they'd hang upside down from the branch of the peach trees, swallowing and exhaling butterflies.

At night, they drew the neon constellations in the sky—Orion, the Venus sisters, Cassiopeia.

Then came the day when they faced each other, their sticks slicing the air.

This was non-contact-combat. Ilona Elek was not struck but blown, as if by a powerful gale, to the ground. She slept as the Pannonian reptiles crawled over her body.

I felt my way back up the hills to the Farkasréti Cemetery and approached the tomb of Ilona Elek. I let her know she had won a gold medal. Banshee, Shoshoah, and Rekas touched me on the nape of my neck, flicked the skin above my lips. This reminded me of the story I was told as a child about the difference between humans and angels. I was mildly annoyed by it. I was trying to escape the angels and they kept coming back, in the form of these intimacies, in the sequences of fencing movements that I inherited from Ilona Elek, and by the secret, two-sticked bat gestures of the old tightrope walker and sword swallower, Tysza Ramkuna.

"I know you like Rekas, but now is not the time to think with your dick," Shoshoah mouthed to me in the Rudas baths, later that night.

I blushed. Yes, I was deeply attracted to them. But I wasn't thinking of it this way.

"Yes, you are," Shoshoah responded telepathically, "but you cannot admit it. You want to consummate your desire for them. But they are coming with us, and for things to work we need to be impersonal."

"But how does desire ruin this?"

"It doesn't always, but for this particular operation it does. You need to hone in on yourself. You need to be in love with all of us."

All day I pined, first for Rekas and then for the loss of my familial roots, until a hurricane spat me from my suburban home in Buda into the gray center of a trembling pine forest. Then leaves shot through my cheeks. Branches sprouted through my torso.

Circumventing the Originary Sphere:
The Rudas Baths (Women's Night)

Yet the river almost seems
To flow backwards, and I
Think it must come
From the east.
—*Frederich Hölderlin*

Had I vomited my last human remnants?
—*Clarice Lispector*

This strange journey—why do I do this, and for what purpose? Banshee told me to go and see for myself. It was a root dissolution voyage, she said: a ritual of dissolving all that was heralded and upheld as the beginning of things. The reproductive lines, the ancestral lines, the cracks in the bark...all must be traced and then dissolved, through a spell I was to recite first in the village square and then by the bartak tree in the forest on the outskirts of town. Then I would leave on the next train, to never return. No more familial pining. No more nationhood pining. No more homeland pining. No more pining. Yet I pined for Shoshoah, Rekas, Ilona, and Banshee—

O, the fellow's wife was bathing opposite me, the only one who was crushworthy, the Clarice Lispector scholar. Her eyes drifted to my direction, but she seemed to look through me, an icy gaze that sent euphoric waves through me. She lent me Lispector's *Agua Viva* to help me understand where I was—in a city filled with thermal water, a city suffused by the Danube—and to help me understand the indifferent nature of the bath spirits.

Do you know what they did to Chaya Clarice Lispector? They tried to capitulate her by going back to her origins—all for the sake of biography. Her mother's rape by the Cossacks, the trauma of the pogroms. But she was all about the "impersonal it." Going beyond the origins of the family, to primal origins, into essential primordial matter, into the cum of the cockroach.

In *The Passion According to G.H*, a bourgeois housewife kills and eats the pus of a cockroach. This encounter sparks a metaphysical epiphany, wherein a humanoid insect perspective unfolds. For it is from this vantage point, Lispector suggests, that we can truly see: see life looking back at us. In this desert of seeing, the human body lies within the cosmic body of the whole—the body that is no longer human. Lispector's Chassidic roots are there, yes, and so are Spinoza's metaphysics, but we do not speak of origins, or of chronological cause. It all happened simultaneously, horizontally: chasidic rupture and the antennae of the cockroach in a fevered circular dance.

I spun around the bath, sending out widening concentric circles while reciting their names. The nymph fountain squirted spring water into my mouth. With the help of Clarice Lispector, I would remake Maya Deren's film in the form of a Transdanubian polymorphic romance. I was near them. I could go there. I was going to work with the Danube Dwellers, the underground beings who smuggled you into deep time. I was going to know Deren through the spirit of the Dacian Queen. My film would become all that there is to know about the history of the unfilmable. It would start here. The CEU was a ghost university, empty wooden conference rooms that led into hallways illuminated by dim lanterns. A bygone era of free education and street activism. There was a sensation of systemic control. The uprising was far away. No escape routes, except those that were imperceptibly forming in the bathhouses and among residents at the cafés. I would call upon the swarm for aid. They would sail us across the Danube, then the Tysa river, before arriving to Transcarpathia, Kryvorivnya. Onwards.

Msg from the Dacian Queen

Beneath the pile of
Paraska's lost pages
lay a faded portrait of the
Dacian queen.
She clicked the aperture

Their noses, beaks
Their arms, wings
Their skin, feathers
Their eye slits of yellow

Owls with horns of gazelle on
their claws Beaks with slits for hungry eyes
Wings with feathers inside out
Feet sliced into potent claws

They walked across Kryvorivnya to
Sibiu From Solotvyno to Sighetu
There were no border guards
No people
No A to B
Bicycles left forlorn
Emptied of Cartesian logic

The shop on the bridge was empty
They filled their pockets w/ Marlboro Reds
Slinging vodka down their throats
Skipping across the border
Then skipping back
One foot in the Ukraine
One foot in Romania
Transcarpathia

ॐ·ૐ·ॐ

In Khust at a Soviet cantine
I saw the Dacian queen in my
borsht soup
Take heed, cried the queen
There are more coming
Gather yourselves into small
groups

Take daggers & mugwort
Scatter yourselves
Don't forget to send in small
troops

Remember to fortify
Fluidify
Become air & feather

Silver shining ones
Don't stare into yr phones
Or you'll freeze

Look closer into this crimson soup
Further away than Transcarpathia
HURL

You see the waitress picking her
nose
She has an envelope with the map
of the uprising (deep inside
her left pocket)

Tip her, ask her politely,
& remember–
"Fuck the Roman empire,
 Fuck Alexander the Great"

Shoshoah blew on my earlobe and woke me from my sulphuric reverie. She silently gestured to the bath's stoned and tiled floor in the cooling pool. I looked down and saw swirling patterns. I lowered my head into the water and dived to the bottom. My hands touched the engravings. I saw *tableux vivants*: a cinematic animation of humans with owl heads accompanied by gazelles, crossing a great river. The gazelles were flying and the owl-humans swam. They appeared to travel as a pack.

I touched these swirling, indented engravings as I noticed a low frequency hum that gradually rose in pitch. I leapt up to the surface of the water and broke it. Shoshoah had vanished. The bath was empty of bathers. There were only pinpricks of light, filtering through the domed roof, which danced across the sur-face of the water.

A Forradalmárok!: The Impersonal lines of Her Face

Shoshoah was imprisoned for three years in Pest before she was bailed out by her comrades at the outbreak of World War I. Her crime: stealing hats from the factory where she had threaded rims since 1911, luxurious hats for the Hapsburg aristocracy, for whom she cut her fingers with the gold plated needles of the infamous Singer machines. They were beautiful machines. She loved the way they gleamed in the drab factory light. But they were badly designed, and the machines got the better of her, jabbing her thumbs with needles. She often laughed with her co-workers to atone for her muteness, and her striking, flashing eyes often drew the attention of the factory boss, who made unwanted advances as she worked late hours. There was a civil war brewing in her community, a class and ideological war. The secular against the religious, the poor against the rich, the anarcho-diasporans against the state-pioneer-Zionists. The conditions of the factory were intolerable. Then there was the uprising, and the factory owners fled to Palestine.

The impersonal lines of Shoshoah's face. I begin to perceive her as though with the optics of Béla Balázs' silent cinema—from a kind of realized mysticism, a macrocosmic world of possibilities. Shoshoah's face emitted impersonal cosmic beauty, in contradistinction to Renée Falconetti's anguished facial expressions in Carl Theodore Dryer's *The Passion of Joan of Arc*. In Dreyer's silent soliloquy the face Joan of Arc, magnified by the extreme close-up of the camera lens, turns into a faceless country, a route out of the land of persecution into the subterranean tunnels and parallel doorways leading to unknown kingdoms and nameless states of being.

Shoshoah's wrinkles are abstract maps to the unknown. I am reading her story to you through the lines and wrinkles of her face. They speak to me of the history of dissident uprisings, the ones in which she participated and the ones her ancestors lived through. To fight, Shoshoah says with a raised eyebrow and a daggered wrinkle, is to go to the picket line and tickle the cops with rose petals.

Bambi Eszpresso Bar is empty. Only the Danube Dwellers look through its panoramic windows. Shoshoah sits close to me and I want to lose myself in her face. She tells me in telepathic form that her face bears the pattern of the Danube and the routes of the migrations of birds. In Bambi, the people next to me are discussing a secret hospital and an ancient cave on the hills of Buda. The Danube Dwellers appear and glare at us through the glass panoramic windows. Their paws scrape the windowpanes, their nails the only solid thing about them. Their faces are not really faces, but protruding, melting beaks, a kind of bird in the making. Shoshoah turns toward me. Pay attention, she says.

Zikr-Zkrun-Emlékezet: Recapitulations Under Water

They instruct me to take a deep breath and hold it in while they pressed my head under the water.

"Because self-pity can transform into anger and anger into hardness and hardness into control and control into a violence and violence into a blocking of the soul."

On this path to healing, I salvage the maps, lucid fragments from unresolved histories. But the event itself exceeded its mark and the person in question multiplied in a kinship with many. I lay under the water and let the sulphate bubbles enter into me.

"You're a porous being. Just a thread away from the Dacian queen. And even closer to Gül Baba and the uprising."

Ilona Elek and Rekas had the same gait as my Aikido teacher, who is dead. I can see their double, their ethereal form as they step in and out of their movements. The sweeping sound of the feet, now slightly off the ground, now silent.

Hooves, feet.

Their heads rotate as if their necks were soft spinning wheels. Around and around, three hundred and sixty degrees.

"Let's recall the recent events that marked your heart. Stay under water."

"Oy vez ez mir!"

There is laughter in the bathhouse.

ठ·ॐ·ठ

You're the spirited, guerilla dreamer
I met sometime in 1942
We were sent to Sachsenhausen you & I
You for joining the Red Orchestra Resistance, me for my
Judenkeit I'd cry outto you from the cell,
you'd throw me breadcrumbs
With secret miniature engravings
A celestial tongue
utterly obscure to the fascists

This filled me with ravenous energy
A peculiar appetite for the flight
& we rolled into the forest
Hiding in the trucks of burnt corpses
Fleeing & barefoot we reached the secret hut
& they were all there
All of them
Chaya, Shoshoah, Rekas, Ilona, Banshee—
Suddenly we were free
A country where everything was permitted
But we were angry and exhausted

While I fixed your wounds
You told me everything

All that was haunting you
I promised to meet you
And that meeting in Paris
On the first day of spring
I fasted before
Hadn't slept for days
Light-headed & elated
I ran towards you
Then the rupture
Words create worlds
Words destroy worlds

In my dream your eyes were glazed over
It was you with a membrane
Skin dressed over skin
If I could just burst the vacuum
Find a way out
Things became volatile
& we were running

The streets were on fire
The cars overturned
The fascists chased us & began to beat the crowd
Then the future with a whimsical, thunderous soundtrack

We fell into a whaling ship
Just like our escape in 1616
We leaped into the whale's coarse throat

There were others but they were already chewed up
Their limbs tossed into the beast's great belly
You fixed my wounds & told me a story
It was about your journey into the desert
Where you learned to talk to gazelles
Oh you mean the gazelles that we met in the Judean desert?
Yes, those ones, but also a very different species
Ones that you can only find in the depths of New Mexico
For when you truly see the deer
They take on another shape from what they once were.
Transparent mammals contain microscopic truths of songs
that were sung Centuries upon centuries before the time of
humanity

"What's the Plan?"
Chaya means life
—*Agua Viva*—stream of life
Do you know that the world exists to discharge her?
& all these women
Those for whom you lived
Gave me the audacity to revive
Her, & the others
More ghostly than a Vishniac portrait
Your hair reached the length of your hips, your eyes glistened
Where the sheep stand between a Transcarpathian town square
On a Friday evening, before the Sabbath
While Hutsul troubadours & Jewish traders
Exchange spice, herbs & live stock

& Maramures' rivers cajole the town square
& Rams' horns blow aquatic melodies

For Chaya, Rekas, shoshoah,
Ilona, Rekas & Banshee For us
&all the others

With the owls perched on our
shoulders
On that cruel liberation day
We were gasping for breath
Starving & feverish & wounded by
The memory of the last encounter
Unforgettable
Sighetu
The town of Elie Wiesel's childhood
Where *Night*'s opening chapter was
staged The stray dogs
& the way your thumb
trembled We noticed
the crimson light The air copper &
sweet Birds circling while you smoked
The rushed beer before crossing the border
"Go to Ukraine?" The old man
grinning & watching We
tried our best
We really did
And you managed to hitch all the way back

While I circled around the town
Looking for loopholes, other dimensions
Maybe it was better not to go back
Not here. No
Not to this time
1943 was bad
2018 was suspiciously sublime
2019 was beautiful
& bleak 1616 was auspicious

& then there was calamity
They beat you down
They ravaged all of you
Left you lying with open wounds
These pogroms, they went
unnoticed No commotion, no
outrage
Just Rekas, Chaya, Shoshoah, Ilona, Banshee & me
Shouting & pulling at their hair
Scraping out the eyeballs
& kicking their nuts in
I would do it for you again and again
& I would murder
Those who hurt you & who try to hurt all of us
We who were on the threshold of escape
& there was the sound of drymba harps & singing
Mugwort dreams & even love making
& the sheep & the mountain moved us

The owl & the deer guarded us
Temporarily transformed
We leapt into another world
Our entire group, surviving & smitten by
The secret, the gazelles' ancient speech

Part Two   The Owl & the Gazelle

Transcarpathian Blues, or Rekas: A Multitude

If you want to know how a shabby, former Soviet café can function as a portal, as a springboard for potential escape—it has something to do with its transparent doorways that face the Danube, and the southern sky. Its red faux-leather chairs, sparsely positioned in the café's center, were intentionally left empty for minds to drift and soften; the position of the actual building and its topographical position towards the stars. Why else would the Danube Dwellers lurk there? It was the only dry place in the city.

The waiter brought me a *palinka.* I had seen the waiter consulting Shoshoah in the private quarter of the café. Shoshoah introduced me to the waiter as Rekas, a trans, Romani musicologist, musician, and DJ who would became a central figure in our growing group. I had the hots for Rekas as soon as I arrived in Bambi. They winked, and seemed to recognize that I wasn't of the heterosexual variety, which was in this city a rare and wonderful thing.

"Your name is Rekas, not Reka?"

"Yes, my name is Rekas. I'm a multitude"

Rekas was plugged into the hum of the bath before any of us were even faintly aware of it. They were down in the sewage tunnels examining the reverb of the drainpipes that summoned the edge of the Bektashi divination melodies. They could replicate the hum on their clarinet with the aid of a delay pedal, and in our group meetings this became a way of maintaining a consistent trance, deterring intrusions from ordinary reality.

Rekas often plugged their clarinet into pedals and distorted the pitch so it became an arpeggiated accompaniment to a parallel Transcarpathian kingdom. E minor: they were in love with that key, and explored it in their work as a scholar of musicology. E minor, Rekas informed me, was a medicinal Klezmer-Roma recipe. It was homeopathic, and if played correctly had the ability to transmute melancholy into ecstatic joy.

We would sit listening to their collection of Transcarpathian blues on the turntable, before their notorious DJ sets at the underground queer nightclub Ököllel, which has since been dismantled by the government. These club nights were a lucid blur of rhapsodic dance and polymorphic dream wave. Syncopated synth lines softened any tension. Bodies became illuminated, inverted forms. Limbs zapped into neon stutters. Rekas' impromptu clarinet interludes oscillated between celestial, rhythmic spurts and languid, earthlike melodies. Stumbling home from these club nights through Pest, arm in arm with Rekas and company, became an active form of revolutionary prophecy.

"Giving a Romani teenager a camera is downright patronizing. I imagine that was your worst film? A dubious compromise of a film?"

"Yes, it was."

It was the worst film that I had ever made, under the aegis of participant ethnography. I sank into my leather booth and downed a palinka in silence. Rekas looked through me and flicked my earlobes.

"What's your next film project?"

"A road movie inspired by Sergei Parajanov's *Shadows of Forgotten Ancestors* and Maya Deren's *Ritual in Transfigured Time.*"

"Now we're talking."

We drew a map of the road trip together. A green line from
Bambi, across the Danube, into the Carpathians: a fairy tale
animated in Technicolour, unfolding in slow motion. All protag-
onists hovering slightly off the ground.

A disembodied camera flies thru a bartak forest, sinking down
into a nest of wild mugwort. Rekas draws an eerie crescent sign
at the gateway to the Carpathians.

"And that's when things need to shift —"

A *Bubópestis* (from the Perspective of Birds)

Budapest is on lockdown, and I'm no longer there. The Danube Dwellers have surrounded Bambi, enshrining it as a protective canopy. Both the dead and a sundry of anomalous beings gather and continue operations on behalf of the living. The living keep dreaming and receiving signals from the dead. There is no lockdown for the dead, or for those between. Shoshoah sits at the threshold. She is like the crowned hoopoe from *The Conference of the Birds*, chirping parables and fables for those with weak hearts. Desire has rerouted itself to another libidinal contour. The organ that is the heart has taken over in unbridled pitch, and Gül Baba leads the sermon.

Once we leave the tomb, we seek shelter in Bambi as the virtual continues expanding across unknown thresholds. The uprising has inversed, hyper-virtualised. Signals have shifted and been heightened; stratospheric infrastructures have been realigned and reformed. The avenue Fő utca unfolds into another spectral kingdom as the Danube Dwellers silently aid the sick and the dying. Subterranean walkways and paths double as stations of underground mutual aid. The birds offer the only feasible form of escape now. Before they were metaphors, but now they are the real thing. When the shit hits the fan, we must turn into birds, Banshee banged the tables of Bambi with her fists. No one disagreed.

The coming of spring brought doves and gazelles, along with a bout of sentimentality and sexual appetite, the very states that I was supposed to transcend in order to rejoin the pack. Not a human soul around. A full reign of bats and owls. Buda looked the most animated it had ever been in plague times. Deer scampered across the empty palace courtyard, oblivious to the fascist state order of Orbán. Further ahead, beyond the derelict tanks and cannons lining the palace tower, the Pannonian lizards crawled down from the Farkasréti Hill and slept on the castle railings. Banshee was there, beside me, as a benevolent night spirit. We sang the Song of Solomon. Flutes and jew harps resounded across the royal grounds, reverberating across the hills, into the wide expanse of the Transylvanian plateau. Buda was biblical Jerusalem, its sister mirrored image, intertwined with histories of Judeo-Islamic chivalry and fraudulent courtship. I roamed the hills that became valleys. I thought of Rekas, their mouth as comely as pomegranate seeds. I thought about Ilona, her neck as smooth as turtle doves. With sachets of myrrh and frankincense in my breasts, the scent of cedarwood in my hair, I finally knocked on their windowpanes. My love pulsated, a purple light that shot into a jasmine flower. It was the spring-filled intention of all springs.

The phantom bathers looked over us, reading us as heterosexual.

I stole through government grounds to plot the explosion. No one noticed me. I strolled surreptitiously into the courtyard, ducked behind the bramble bush by the maze of royal roses that face the Baroque brick tower. The guard even smiled and waved me through.

Rekas, lying in the Király steam room where we squatted, was astounded by my privilege and squandered opportunity. They told me to blow up parliament and not waste any more time during the tourist-free zone of the plague.

"What do you think you were doing, lingering there and parading your wonderful whiteness? Do you think they don't know your ancestors, you green-eyed, curly-haired dyke?"

I loved being called a dyke by them. But I would have preferred being called a kike.

We kissed deeply and drew apart, our feet squelching in the rose steam as we dispersed into the sulphate mist. We left the dynamite in drainpipes, inside the ovens of the bath.

The Bath Philosophers: Secular Visions

If you are looking for childhood reminiscences and familial nar-
ratives, you won't find them here. This is a leap into deep space.
In the Lukács Baths there are signs on the walls that say *A csend
gyógyít,* "silence heals." I learn the art of the silent soliloquy from
the mute Shoshoah, and from the Hungarian film historian, Béla
Balázs. These baths are mostly visited by the local intelligentsia.
The men on either side of me look like Jacques Derrida—a good
philosopher for these times, or a good bath philosopher, since
he summons the spectral, the phantasmagorical glitch of time
leaks. The bath philosopher's silvery heads bob up and down in
the cooled water. Their eyes are focused on some distant detail of
the broken walled tiles. Hands on their face, lost in thought. Not
talking, silently soliloquey-ing. Thought seems to be of a differ-
ent order when they are summoned here. However cerebral you
are, a thought in here is not tied to a thing, nor to an attitude, it
is a troubadour kind of thinking: think Sergei Parajanov's bath
scene in *The Colour of Pomegranates,* the cinematic summoning
of the eighteenth century troubadour poet, Sayat Nova. Recall
the bathers in those medieval Georgian baths, their expressions
of indescribable bliss evoking a homoerotic dreamtime, a sensual
awakening among the communal spirit of the bathers. For it is in
these baths that their minds and bodies can freely cruise. They
dance around the shooting fountain, bodies in malleable, toned,
warrior forms, massaging each other's temples, mouths kissing

the damp floor, knees bent, backs curved over, limbs intertwined, feet rotating counterclockwise on streaming mosaics.

Beyond the minerals of these baths (for it is the minerals that supply their medicinal properties), the water is more than the sum of its parts. It is geological froth. It is the mind's reactionary tendencies softening. Revolutionary thought is at its most potent if you allow yourself to surrender to it. The bath's history, and its present, speak to the water's unnameable healing powers, to the language and speech of the Permian evaporites, the Triassic bedrock between the southern and eastern foot of the Buda and Pilis mountains, discharged via hot springs into the Danube.

The mayor said that sulphites kill the bacteria, but Orbán had a secret plan to seal us in the baths. He said migrants were responsible for the virus. The baths provided the space for solidarity, safety, and sanctuary when they became a place of imperceptibility. There was a potent smell of sulphur, and more steam than I'd ever seen. We held hands under the water. We could see heads bobbing up and down with silvery hair. The bath philosophers instructed us to dive down and read the inscriptions at the bottom of the bath. But the bottom never arrived, and there were floating letters that transformed into fish. We had to shift our bodies into another direction.

Bifocal Freedom (The Screening of Birds)

The floodgates opened up after the film was seen: "Bifocal Freedom," a screening that was a final dirge to old, anarchist Budapest before chains bolted the borders and protest ground to a halt, as the last student left for Austria with the hope of a more subtle imperialist existence among the Hapsburg shadows. The films of András Szirtes, a banned troubadour poet, were screened with the aim of forging a portal into another world. A spectacular form of prophetic fragments projected in grainy black and white before a bemused audience at the CEU auditorium became a magical rite and unlocked a parallel world among the ruins of the city. The floodgates opened: floodgates of primordial origin, memories and experiences of those whose lives with whom I became entangled in a act of collective recapitulation. Eagle-owls sat perched on the front row seats, where there were also a great many elderly women wrapped in furs. The eagle-owls fluttered their wings. Then, in an alchemy of filmstock, nitrate celluloid, and digital glitch, András Szirtes' sublime 16mm film, *Madarak*: a cinematic study of the birds of Budapest gliding in flocks over the Danube at night, of diasporic migration. Delirious spirals over the Danube. A crescent moon illuminating the beaks. The old ladies, who looked like glamorous holocaust survivors in their fur coats, were moved to tears. We waited, collectively, for the chime of the bell to announce the end of the screening.

The velvet curtain fell, and I drifted into the Danube, naked and determined to journey into the Carpathians. What night will herald this love, prehistoric and futuristic? What night?

Part Three   Out Takes: *Into the Carpathians*

Scenes from a Dunghill

Why so many partisans in the forest?
The link between pantheistic rapture
& revolution,
Chassidic suicide and sexual bliss?

Was I being a pragmatic bitch
Or did I seek something more than
the sum of these parts?

The rest of them were waiting for us on a concealed plateau in a forested glade in western Ukraine. We weren't far from Kryvorivnya.

Shoshoah unrolled a huge map with the flows of the Danube and the Tysa marked across the Transdanubian basin. Pink dots and neon green lines zigzagged across the page in delirious flight.

András Szirtes ruffled his long grey hair across the map, as crow feathers fell from his head onto the lines and contours of the great, ruffled paper.

Ilona Elek imitated a sprinting gazelle with her glistening sword. The sword became the head of the animal, her fists its ears, her bottom its ass. Her legs multiplied and she became a duplicate of the gazelle that I watched in the parks of my child-hood. She sprinted gayly, gently slicing her sword through the air. I longed to dance with her, and drew slowly toward her. She gently speared me on my chin, tickling my face. I lost balance. So this is how she wins her matches, I thought, as my body fell silently to the mossy ground.

We must practice the gazelle's walk, its sprint, if we are to find each other. We need to learn its language.

We rode a pack of horses up the luminous, soft crevice. It could have been the early 1900s, but it was impossible to know in this vortex of the western Carpathians. The sounds of birds were occasionally interrupted by an electronic pulse that flashed through the air and caused its inhabitants to sing, with a guttural depth that issued from their small bellies, a most majestic form of sing song they learned from boars. With their mud-ridden, mauve bodies and sensual, anomalous snouts, the boar were certainly the most attractive of all species in these parts,.

Hadigria, the handsomest of boars, adorned with the pearls and twigs of the Tysza and the tadpoles and worms of its ponds, waddled furtively towards Rekas, the most beautiful among the humans. Rekas blushed in delight as the hog let out a seductive snort and danced a spontaneous circle jig around us. We clapped and, sure enough, the entirety of life inhabiting this crevice joined in raucously, singing in E minor.

What could have been a subtropical storm glowed with purple light behind the Carpathians, fading into restless pines. The owls chose to confine themselves to their nests until the turbulence subsided. What had they heard from the top of the precipice? Not raven, not eagle-owl. Their ears were keen enough to question whether it was birdsong at all, or whether it was something entirely other. From the sweet, dewy air they could pick up the pungent scent of pure, embodied desire that swarmed through the atmosphere like hornets or bees. This desire had no recognizable shape or form in its alien contours. Perhaps even naming it desire was not entirely accurate. They could sense something lingering, beyond the ordinary hunter-gatherer routine, something softer and less distinct than instinct.

The horses now freely roamed the forested meadow, neighing in fits and starts. Something was in the air, they said. Now all of us agreed. All inhabitants of this enclave were in agreement. Banshee yelped from across the trees. Ilona Elek struck her sword into the rock. Rekas skirted across the dungheap. Shoshoah floated through the river.

Then a branch, and more branches fell with rhapsodic determination. Piles of wood began to rub against each other. A fire caught, licked, and erupted. Night fell suddenly, and without warning. There was no time to recline in the moss as sounds began to reverberate across the crevice, a low frequency hum.

Fissures deepened across the faces of dead and fallen leaves.
What had begun in previous centuries now resumed. In the pines
a shadow grew, and we saw the swarm, waiting for us to murmur.

▽ ▽ ▽   The Danube river flows through Slovakia, Hungary, Romania, and Ukraine, spilling back in time, into the Dacian empire, the Samaritan and Socratic lines, all the way across Galicia, the kingdom of Hungary, and the Hapsburg empire.

▽ ▽ ▽   One midsummer's night, on the edge of an inconspicuous brook, the Tysa River flees the Danube, overlooked by the Carpathian forest. It brims with the rocks of an exploded, pre-historic volcano.

▽ ▽ ▽   A queen leaves a pearl on the foot of a precipice. A shepherd's delight.

▽ ▽ ▽   The window rips open. A Hutsul elder describes the sensation of a blue, hot wind. A shadow dances around the old man's wooden table.

▽ ▽ ▽   Beyond the contours of a people, of a tribe, a nation—beyond the flocks of cattle, the flow of rivers and the migration of birds—there flies the night spirits.

▽ ▽ ▽   Once an eagle-owl flew through the valleys of Transcarpathia, a gazelle's horn hanging from its claws.

▽ ▽ ▽   There was a silent swoop as the owl landed on the hills of Kryvorivnya.

▽ ▽ ▽   Threshold crossings. Look—the vampires mid-flight!

Acknowledgments

I am grateful to Daniel Pini for reading back the raw manuscript to me aloud every night by the volcano. Thank you to my loving and courageous parents Robbie and Sally Schiendel, and to my supportive sibling Rafe. Grateful to Meg John Barker for their in-depth feedback, consultation, and encouragement. I deeply appreciate the feedback and support of my ally Scott Thurston, to whom I can always trust and find inspiration. Thanks to Barry Schwabsky, Haytham el Wardany, and Jesse Darling for their generous reading and feedback on a raw draft. Greatly appreciate the presence and support of Ziggy Devriendt, who believed in the musical side of this project. Deep thanks to Julian Talamentez Brolaski for its consistent warmth, love and profound alliance whose presence secretly accompanied me through the process of this writing. Grateful to Oleksandr Debych whose hospitality and generous guidance across Transcarpathia and the Carpathians built the very foundations for me to dream and explore. I am incredibly fortunate to have this work land in Broc Rossell's hands, and thank them for their magical collaboration on this writing and for believing in it. Thank you Enir Da, my partner in crime, whose musical accompaniment always takes me further across the edge.

Fragments of this book have previously appeared as lyrics on *Dali Muru & The Polyphonic Swarm*'s debut album released on Stroom in January 2022, and as a storytelling hour on NTS radio show broadcast in February 2022.

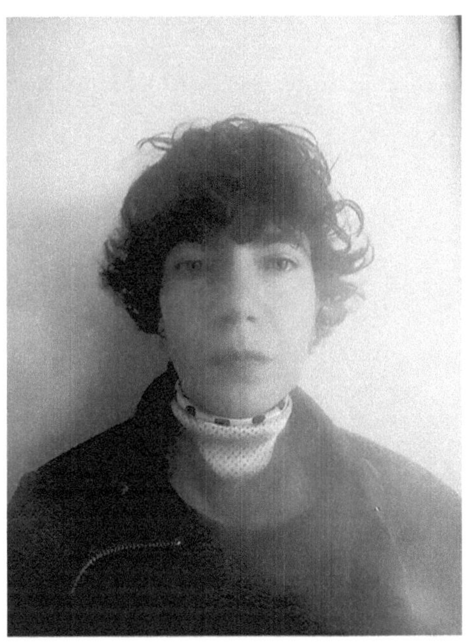

Dalia Neis is a writer, filmmaker, and musician living in Berlin. Previous publications include *Zephyrian Spools: An Essay, a Wind* (Knives, Forks & Spoons), and *Hercules Road* (MA Bibliothèque). Dalia is also lyricist and vocalist for *Dali Muru & The Polyphonic Swarm*.

9 781639 551040